Disney · PIXAR

BRAVE

One Brave Lady

ISBN: 978-1-338-12831-4

10 9 8 7 6 5 4 3 2 1   16 17 18 19 20

Printed in Malaysia 106

First Printing, September 2016

Scholastic Inc.

Here comes the princess!
Her hair is as red as a **flame**.

Her **name** is Merida.
And she is very **brave**!

Merida must **train** to be a **lady**.
But she **hates** to **paint**.

She **hates** to **play** music.

She **hates** to **stay** in the castle all **day**.

Her parents **say** she must
change her **ways**.

She must marry the winner
of the royal **game**!

But Merida is **brave**.

She wants to **change** her **fate**.

Merida **raises** her hand.

She will **play** in the **game**.

Merida **takes aim**.

She wins the **game**!

Merida is one **brave lady**.